MW01155322

To:

From:

Date:

Bedtime Read and Rhyme

BIBLE STORIES

Bonnie Rickner Jensen
Illustrated by Robert Dunn

Tommy Nelson®
A Division of Thomas Nelson Publishers

Bedtime Read and Rhyme Bible Stories

Published in Nashville, Tennessee, by Tommy Nelson. Tommy Nelson is an imprint of Thomas Nelson. Thomas Nelson is a registered trademark of HarperCollins Christian Publishing, Inc.

Tommy Nelson titles may be purchased in bulk for educational, business, fund-raising, or sales promotional use. For information, please e-mail SpecialMarkets@ThomasNelson.com.

ISBN-13: 978-0-7180-8834-7

Library of Congress Cataloging-in-Publication Data is on file.

Printed in China

16 17 18 19 20 DSC 6 5 4 3 2 1

Mfr: DSC / Shenzhen, China / October 2016 / PO # 9399761

Your love is so great it
reaches to the skies.

Psalm 57:10

Old Testament Stories

New Testament Stories

A Letter to Parents

My prayer while raising three daughters was that they would not simply learn about Jesus, but that they would fall in love with Him. I wanted Him to become as real as their first friend at school and as comforting as their favorite blanket. I also wanted them to know that the stories in the Bible are as true as the God who inspired them.

I hope that as you read this book you encounter the love and joy of the Spirit of God from beginning to end. Part of that joy is in the rhyme of the words, knowing that when reading to a child, rhythm makes it more fun—and memorable.

Also, a promise brought to life through story is a powerful way to open hearts, both young and old, to truth and understanding. Jesus spoke in parables, knowing how story allows us to relate the promises of God to our own lives and circumstances.

The story of a boy named David is going to resonate with the child who wants to believe they have the courage to do *anything* with God on their side. The story of Gideon will remind every child that God chooses even the small and weak to do great things. And the story of Esther will help children understand how God works everything together with timing and wisdom in order to carry out His perfect plan.

I pray this happy, hopeful, fun-to-read book of Bible stories will make its way into the heart of every child who hears or reads it, and that children will realize they're a lot like the people they're learning about—valued, forgiven, loved, and chosen.

—Bonnie Rickner Jensen

Listen, people of Israel! The Lord is our God. He is the only Lord. Love the Lord your God with all your heart, soul and strength. Always remember these commands I give you today. Teach them to your children. Talk about them when you sit at home and walk along the road. Talk about them when you lie down and when you get up.

—Deuteronomy 6:4-7

Old Testament Stories

God's Creation, Our Home

Genesis 1

The earth had no shape,
No order or light . . .
Covered in darkness
With no life in sight.
Then God, the Creator,
Began His great plan—
To make it our home,
With a mighty command:
"Let there be light!"
And so it was so!
The time had come
For nothingness to go.

The light made God happy,
But He wasn't done.
The light and the darkness
Were two things, not one.
So dark became night,
And light became day.
Creation's beginning
Was well underway!
A sky that was endless
And painted true blue
Was set above waters
Below on day two.

Bedtime Prayer
Dear God, when I look at all You created,
I'll remember how much You love me.

Next came the seas,
The grass, and the trees.
All this was good,
God saw on day three.
He scattered the stars,
Hung the moon in its place.
["The sun is for *you* . . .
Feel the warmth on your face?"]
God filled up the oceans
And decorated the sky,
Where the fish now swim
And the birds fly high!

Then came the animals,
The wild and the tame,
To wander the earth
And be blessed in His name.
They galloped and hopped,
Scurried and soared,
Chirped and barked,
Howled and roared!
God looked with a smile
At all He had done.
Then His heart looked
Forward to *you*, little one.

Adam and Eve Go from Happy to Sad

Genesis 2–3

At last it was time
For God's best to begin,
Made in His image,
As child and friend.

Adam and Eve were
Made by God's hand,
To live and to rule
In this beautiful land.

He planted a garden
And made it their home,
A happy and wonderful
Place to roam.

Eden was bursting with
Every good thing:
Animals, flowers,
Birds to sing.

The fruit became sweet
From the beams of the sun.
God said, "Eat freely
From all trees but one."

Adam and Eve
Followed God's simple rule.
Together they walked
When the day became cool.

One day God came down
And called Adam by name.
He found that His children
Were hiding in shame.

"We feel something's wrong,"
Adam answered in fear.
God knew why His children
Were scared to come near.

His enemy, Satan,
Had told Eve a lie—
Disguised as a snake,
He was clever and sly.

"Eat from this tree.
It will open your eyes!
You'll know good from bad,
And like God, you'll be wise."

With one bite they knew
That God's warning was true.
Not listening to Him
Was the *worst* thing to do.

"You must leave the garden,
But I won't leave you.
I'll love you and watch
Over all that you do."

God's heart was broken
To send them away.
He knew that their lives
Would be harder each day.

Sadly, the snake had
Brought more than a lie.
The poison of sin
Would cause all things to die.

But God's love is bigger—
As big as the sky!
It wins over death!
It squashes the lie!

Love will rise up;
This will not be the end.
God has a plan
That will save us from sin.

Bedtime Prayer

Dear God, thank You for Your love that is as big as the sky!

The Ark, the Rain, and the Rainbow

Genesis 6–9

God had filled the earth with life,
Created out of love.
Noah understood that God
Was watching from above.

In time God saw His people choose
To turn from good to bad.
Evil spread throughout the land.
God's heart was very sad.

But Noah was a special man
Who walked with God each day.
So God asked him to build an ark,
And he chose to obey.

The ark was long and tall and wide,
A mighty ship of wood.
Noah listened faithfully
And made it as he should.

"I'll bring a flood upon the land!"
God said to Noah's heart.
"I'll save you and your family too.
Your faith sets you apart."

"I'll call the creatures, two by two,
Each animal and bird.
Every creeping, crawling thing
Will enter at My word."

The rain came down at God's command
For forty days and nights!
Many months the great ark sailed
With no dry land in sight.

Noah and his family had
So many things to do.
Imagine taking care of
An entire floating zoo!

Bedtime Prayer

Dear God, help me trust
You every day.

Finally, the time had come
For all the drops to stop.
God sent a mighty wind to blow—
Out peeked the mountaintops!

Noah held a dove in hand,
Releasing it to fly.
Soon it brought an olive leaf
To prove the earth was dry.

God made a promise He would keep,
And with it came a sign:
"The rainbow will remind Me
Of these words for all of time."

"I'll never flood the earth again,
For all I say is true—
A rainbow in the clouds will mean
I'm faithful, child, to you."

The Proud Tower

Genesis 11

In time the earth was filled with folks.
They all had different faces,
Different voices, different smiles—
But weren't in different places.

One language kept them in one spot,
And so they came up with a plot
To build and build until they got
A tower to the sky!

"We're smart enough!
We're strong enough!
We have the plans;
We have the stuff!"
God saw them in their
Prideful huff and
Came down in a hurry.

"Together they are full of pride.
They'll do whatever they decide—
Forget they need Me by their side."
And so He stopped their plans.

He scattered them
From here to there,
He gave them speech
They couldn't share,
He left the tower
In midair—reminding them,
"You're in My care."

Bedtime Prayer
Dear God, I pray my heart does not get too proud!

Abram, a Blessed Man of God

God's Plan for Abram

Genesis 12

Long ago
And far away,
Abram took the
Time to pray.
God said, "I will
Bless your life,
But you must leave
Now with your wife."

"I'll show you where
You need to go,
And when you get there,
You will know
That Canaan is
The land for you,
And all of your
Descendants too."

Abram's life was
Greatly blessed,
And he found out
It's always best
To follow what
God says to do—
It's how you'll know
His plan for *you*!

Bedtime Prayer

Dear God, only You know what's best. I want to follow Your good plans for me!

Bedtime Prayer

Dear God, help me believe Your promises. even when I'm sad.

Starry Night, Promise Bright

Genesis 15, 17

Abram's heart was thankful
For the things that God had done.
But still, he hoped for children,
And he told God, "I have none."

God said, "Abram, go outside,
And look up at the sky.
See if you can count the stars!
Let Me tell you why."

"Your family will be many,
Like the stars you see tonight.
You'll have a child with your wife
When the time is right."

Abram became *Abraham*,
And God said, "You will see!
You'll father nations, even kings,
If you believe in Me."

Bedtime Prayer
Dear God, thank You for keeping Your promises!

God of the Impossible

Genesis 18, 21

Abraham believed
God's promise—
He would have a son!
But Sarah laughed
And thought,
I don't know how
It can be done.

You see, she knew their
Time had passed
To have a baby boy.
It would take a miracle
For them to feel that joy!

But our God has no limits.
He'll do what can't be done!
Abraham and Sarah finally
Welcomed their own son.

Isaac means "he laughed,"
And laughter
Comes with joy!
God had kept His
Promise with this
Brand-new baby boy.

A Special Bride for Isaac

Genesis 24

Abraham taught Isaac
Of God's faithfulness
And truth.
Isaac's life was blessed
And favored,
Even in his youth!

Isaac grew into a man,
And so the time
Had come;
Abraham told
His servant,
"You must find the one."

"Someone from my
Homeland will be
Isaac's chosen bride.
I'll pray God sends
An angel first,
To help you to decide!"

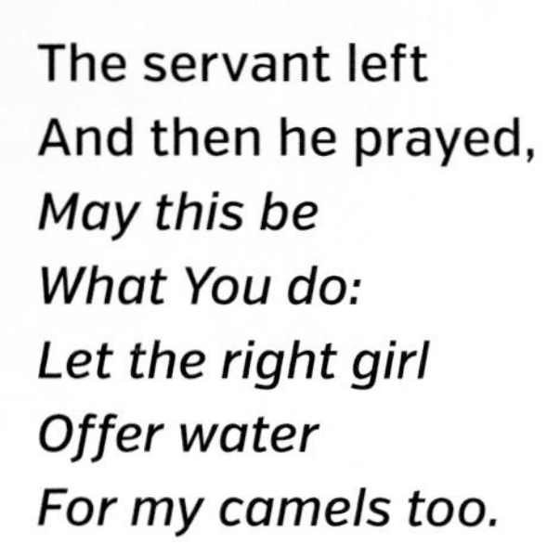

The servant left
And then he prayed,
May this be
What You do:
Let the right girl
Offer water
For my camels too.

A kind girl named Rebekah
Came to share
Her water jar.
"I'll bring some
For your camels too"
(For they had traveled far).

Rebekah let the
Camels drink
Until they all were done.
The servant's heart
Was happy now—
He knew she was the one!

Dear God, thank You for hearing my prayers and showing me what to do each day.

Jacob Dreams of a Ladder

Genesis 28

Isaac prayed God
Would give them a son.
He did, and Rebekah
Had two boys, not one!
Jacob and Esau,
Different as can be,
Grew up together.
But Jacob would flee.

He traveled as far
As he could for the day.
Nighttime had come,
So there he would stay.
I wonder . . . is *your*
Pillow soft for your head?
Jacob laid his
On a stone instead!

During his sleep,
God gave him a dream,
A ladder as tall
As the tallest sunbeam.
It sat on the earth
And reached to the sky.
The angels walked on it,
It stood so high!

Jacob awoke from his dream
With a start.
He knew God was speaking
A word to his heart.
"I'm with you right now
And wherever you go.
This land will be yours,
And your family will grow!"

The news put a smile
On Jacob's face.
He said, "I know God
Is here in this place!"
He took the stone
(His pillow that night)
And stood it up
To mark the site.

Then Jacob poured oil
On top of the stone
And said, "God lives here!
Let this be known!"
He learned God is good,
And He's good to *you* too!
Wherever you go
And whatever you do.

Bedtime Prayer

Dear God, I'm happy You're with me wherever I go.

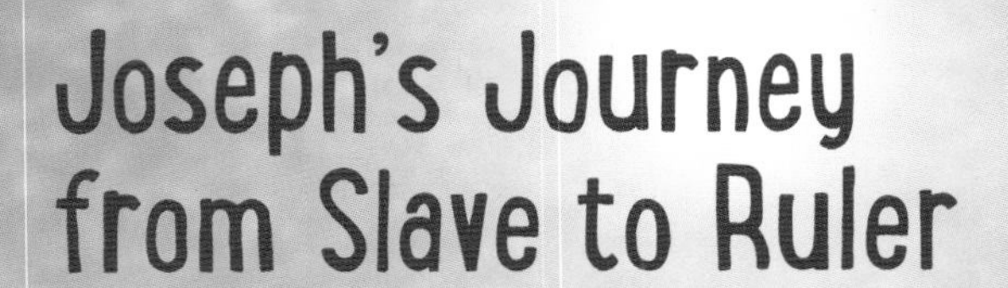

Joseph's Journey from Slave to Ruler

Genesis 37–45

In time, Jacob had
Twelve strapping sons!
In his old age came
His favorite one.
His name was Joseph,
And as he grew,
His brothers would
Hate him because they knew . . .

Jacob showed favor
To Joseph each day.
He made him a coat—
A colorful display!
His brothers were mad
And began to say,
"We'd like our young
Brother to go away."

To make things worse,
Joseph shared his dream . . .
"One day you'll bow down
To me, it would seem."
Now more than ever
They wanted him gone.
Their anger would lead them
To do something wrong.

Joseph was sent to
His brothers one day.
His father said, “Go and
Make sure they’re okay.”
Joseph said *yes*
And obeyed as he should.
Soon he would know
He was leaving for good.

His brothers were watching
The sheep as they ate.
They saw Joseph coming
And filled up with hate.
They tore off his colorful
Coat right away,
Then threw him down into
A well, where he’d stay.

While they were eating,
Some traders passed by.
“Let’s sell our young
Brother, and tell him good-bye!”
And so, Joseph went from
A son to a slave,
But God would go with him
And help him be brave.

Joseph worked hard
And his master could see,
Wherever he was
God's blessing would be!

And so he made Joseph
His head of household.
Then Joseph was blamed
For a lie that was told.

He didn't do wrong,
But to prison he went!
Then men came to ask
About dreams that God sent.

One night the great pharaoh
Woke up from a dream
Of fat cows and skinny cows.
What did it mean?

He called for Joseph,
Who knew what to say—
Then Joseph was let out
Of prison that day!

The dreams God sent Pharaoh
Meant hard times would come . . .
Seven years of food,
Then seven years of none!

Joseph became ruler,
Just as God planned,
Then stored lots of food
For people in his land.

His brothers came to Egypt,
For they were hungry too.
Joseph knew them right away
And told them, "I forgive you."

Joseph had God's love inside;
It showed him how to be.
When *you* are kind to others,
God's love is what they see!

Bedtime Prayer

Dear God, You keep me strong and bring good things out of the hard things in my life.

Moses Leads God's People

A Mommy Saves Her Son

Exodus 1–2

God told Jacob
His family would grow.
And *wow*—it grew and grew!
The pharaoh in Egypt
Was scared of God's people.
He thought of a bad thing to do.

"When a Hebrew boy is born,
Do not let him live.
I am the leader! I am the boss!
This is the order I give."

When Moses was born,
His mommy created
A basket to be like a boat.
She put Moses inside
(A good place to hide),
And then she set it afloat.

His sister watched
And saw that the basket
Was not in the river
For long.
Pharaoh's daughter
Saw Moses and thought,
With me is where you belong.

Bedtime Prayer
Dear God, thank You for the ones who love and care for me every day.

Pharaoh's daughter
Saw Moses crying,
And this is what she knew:
Sending his sister
To find him a nurse
Is what she had to do.

That nurse was his mommy!
But no one else knew.
In her care, he grew and grew.
She felt that God had a
Greater plan—something
Special for Moses to do.

When he was older, she
Told Pharaoh's daughter,
"Now he must stay with you."
She kissed him good-bye
And prayed to God,
I'm trusting my son to You.

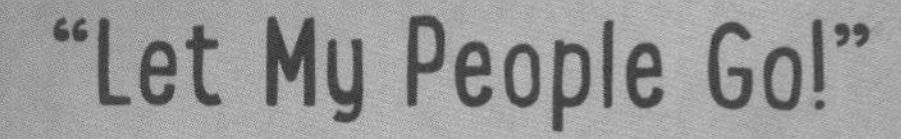

"Let My People Go!"

Exodus 1, 3–14

Moses grew into a big, strong man
And saw that God's people were sad.
When Moses took time to help a slave,
Pharaoh was very mad!

Pharaoh decided that Moses should die,
So Moses ran away.
He went to a place where he felt safe,
And that's where he chose to stay.

One day, when Moses was in the desert,
He saw a bush filled with flames.
The fire was burning, red and hot,
But the bush was staying the same!

God's voice thundered from inside the bush,
"It's time for Pharaoh to know.
Go back to Egypt and say to him,
'Let My people go!'"

Moses went to Egypt,
Like God told him to do.
But Pharaoh's ears refused to hear
That God was strong or true.

Our God is real and cannot lie,
So He told Moses to reply:
"Pharaoh, let My people go!
Or I'll do things to let you know
That I am God, and I am here.
I'll make My presence very clear!"

Sadly, Pharaoh's heart was cold,
And he kept saying, "No, no, *no*!"
So God sent frogs and bugs and hail
Till all the land began to wail.

Then Pharaoh saw that God's might
Was something that He couldn't fight.
He said to Moses, "Set them free!
Take God's people far from me!"

The Israelites
Marched out of sight,
Through the day
And through the night.
God would guide them
With His love
And send a cloud
From up above.

The cloud was shade
From desert sun,
Then turned to fire
When day was done.
The people knew
That God was there,
And they felt safe now,
In His care.

But when they reached
The great Red Sea,
Their hearts were
Filled with fear.
Pharaoh had come
After them,
And he was very near!

But God is good,
And God is true.
He split the water
Right in two!
They learned how
God can make a way.
His love can always
Save the day!

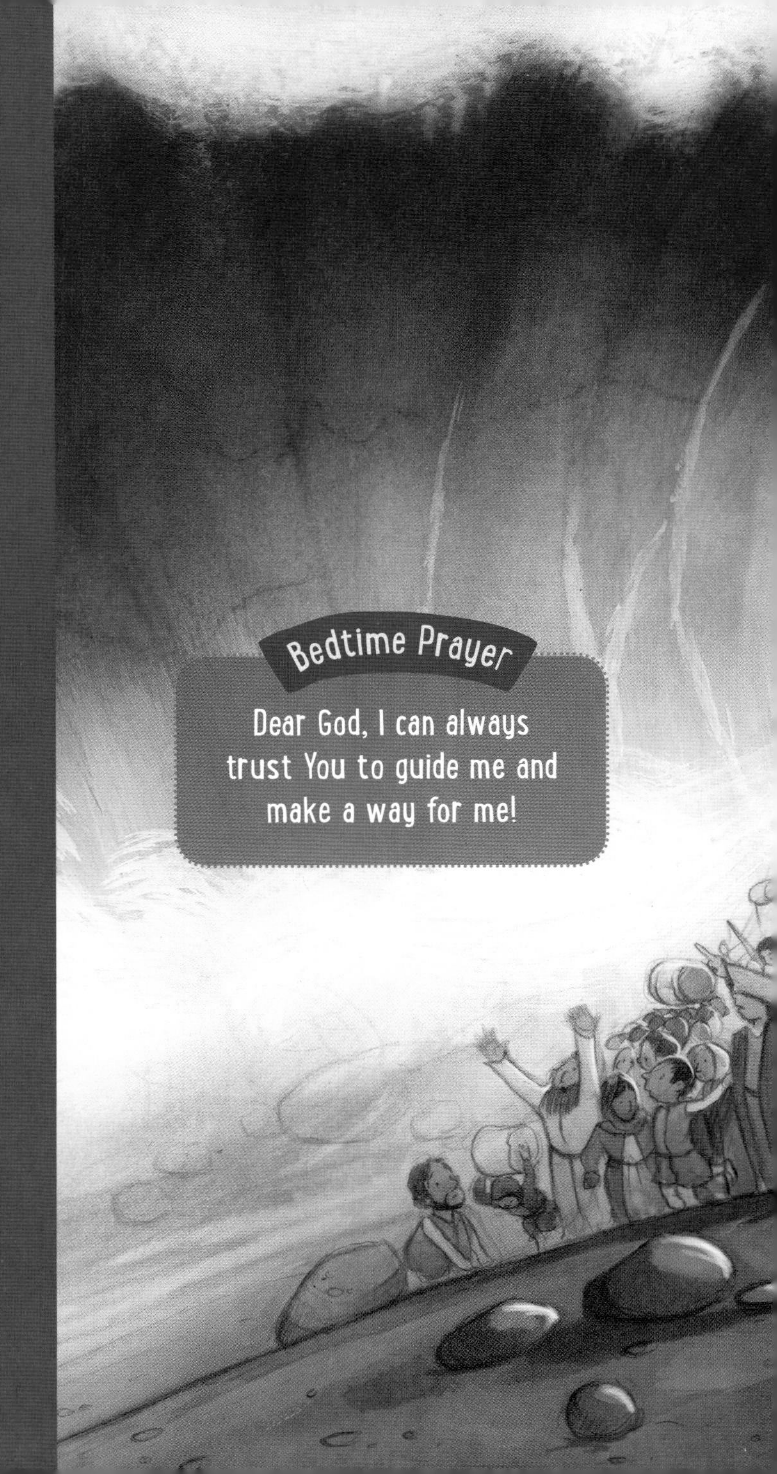

Bedtime Prayer

Dear God, I can always trust You to guide me and make a way for me!

Bread from Heaven and God's Good Rules

Exodus 16, 20

God's people were happy.
They sang and cheered!
They knew God had saved them
From all they feared.

But in time they grew hungry
And grumbly, and so . . .
They went to Moses
To let him know.

God told Moses,
"I'll rain down bread!
Obey Me and trust Me.
I'll keep you fed!"

God filled their tummies
Day after day.
Do *you* thank Him for food
When you pray?

Bedtime Prayer

Dear God, thank You for taking care of my needs and teaching me right from wrong.

God loves His people
With all of His heart.
He loves to protect
Them too.
So He said to Moses,
“I’ll come to Mount Sinai,
To give My rules to you.”

The Ten Commandments
He gave for our good—
They help us live
The way we should!
Love God
And worship Him alone.
Use His name
In a loving tone.

Make the Lord’s day
Special to you.
Honor your parents
In all you do.
Do not lie, steal, or kill.
If you marry,
Your promise, fulfill.
When others are blessed,
Be happy inside!
Thank You, God.
Your love is our guide!

Joshua Marches Through Jericho

Joshua 5–6

The Israelites were almost there,
Where God told them they'd be.
It was Joshua's time to lead—
Brave and strong was he!

The land that God had promised them
Was such a wonderful place.
But standing right before them
Was a city they must face.

Jericho was locked up tight.
No one could come or go!
With walls so thick, strong, and tall,
Joshua needed to know:

"How will we do this?
How will we win?
How, with these walls,
Will we ever get in?"

So God sent an angel
With a sword in hand.
"The city is yours, Joshua,
Just as God planned."

Bedtime Prayer

Dear God, I can be brave every day because You are with me.

What God said to do
Might sound silly to you,
But Joshua was ready to hear.
He listened to God
With his brave, strong heart,
Obeying without any fear.

"March once 'round the city
Six days in a row.
On the seventh day,
Seven times you'll go.
Then tell My people
To let out a shout!
The bricks will tumble!
The walls will give out!"

"You'll march right through
The city that day—
Right foot, left foot,
On your way!
Around the desert
You'll no longer roam.
Finally, My children,
You'll have your new home."

God Chooses Gideon

Judges 6–7

God's people needed help again—
That's when God called Gideon.
He said, "Oh Lord, my clan is weak,
And I'm the least of all.
But if You say You're with me,
I will answer this great call!"

God said, "I'll be with you,
And we will win this fight.
My people will be sure it's Me—
It won't be by *your* might!"

Gideon's army,
Small and weak,
Didn't run and hide.
They won their land
From a great big army.
God was on their side!

If ever you were thinking
God will choose only the best—
The ones who are much
Stronger or much greater
Than the rest . . .
This story about Gideon
Must be a big surprise!
God will choose
What's right for *you*—
He is very wise!

Bedtime Prayer

Dear God, thank You for making me for a special purpose.

Ruth and Naomi's New Start

Ruth 1–4

God gives us friends
Who are special and true.
Sometimes our best friends
Are family too!

Naomi was happy
With who God would send:
Her daughter-in-law, Ruth,
Was a very good friend.

Naomi had lost
Her husband and sons.
Sadly, she felt that
Her good days were done.

But Ruth told Naomi,
"I'll never leave you.
I'll go where you go,
And I'll always be true."

They traveled together
To Bethlehem,
Where a man named
Boaz took them in.

Boaz and Ruth
Became man and wife.
Both were good people,
And God blessed their life.

In time God would give them
A son of their own.
Naomi knew this was
How God's love was shown.

She held baby Obed
With joy in her heart.
She thanked God for giving
Them all a new start!

Bedtime Prayer

Dear God, with You, I have hope for good things to come!

Bedtime Prayer
Dear God, thank You for listening to my prayers.

A Prayer from Hannah's Heart

1 Samuel 1

God hears our prayers
The moment we start,
Listening to our voices,
Seeing our hearts.

Hannah's heart hurt,
For she wanted a son.
Years went by . . .
Still she had none.

One day a priest saw her
Praying in tears.
He blessed her and said,
"Go in peace, without fear."

Hannah felt happy.
Her face was bright too.
She smiled, looking forward
To what God would do.

God is so good.
He gave Hannah a son!
She named the boy Samuel,
Saying, "Look what God's done!"

Samuel, God's Good Listener

1 Samuel 1–3

Hannah loved Samuel
With all of her heart.
She knew he was chosen
By God from the start.

So while he was only
A very young boy,
He went to serve God,
And it gave Hannah joy!

Eli, the priest who had
Heard Hannah's prayer,
Welcomed young Samuel
Into his care.

Samuel spent time
In the temple with God,
Serving and praying
Each day.
Then one night God
Called to him
In an unusual way.

Samuel heard his name
Out loud.
He ran to Eli and said,
"Here I am!"
But Eli answered,
"It wasn't me.
Go back to bed."

A second time
Samuel heard his name,
So he ran to Eli's side.
"Here I am!
You called to me."
Eli said, "I've not
Even tried!"

After three times,
Eli knew—Samuel was
Hearing *God's* call.
He told Samuel,
"Answer Him, son.
God's word is the
Greatest of all!"

Bedtime Prayer

Dear God, thank You for giving me the Bible to read. It's filled with Your words for me!

David, Young and Mighty King

Samuel Blesses the Littlest Son

1 Samuel 16

God kept speaking to Samuel.
Samuel listened to God's voice.
God wanted Israel to have the *right* king—
He sent Samuel to find His choice.

God said, "Go to Bethlehem.
The new king is Jesse's son.
Of the eight sons he brings to you,
I will show you who is the one."

Seven fine-looking sons passed by,
But none were meant to be king.
Samuel looked at Jesse and said,
"Do you have no more sons to bring?"

"There's one more son, a shepherd boy."
"Send for him!" Samuel said.
When David came forward,
God told Samuel,
"By him, My people will be led."

God chose David to be the king—
The youngest brother of all!
David's heart was willing to serve
And ready to answer God's call.

Samuel rose to bless the boy,
As God had told him to do:
"From this day on, young David,
God's power will be with you!"

Bedtime Prayer

Dear God, You bless those who follow You. Thank You for blessing me!

The Boy and the Giant

1 Samuel 17

God's power stayed with David.
He grew strong and had no fear.
The strength of God was with him—
Very soon it would be clear!

He was still a shepherd
When his brothers went to fight.
God's people faced a giant,
And their hearts were filled with fright!

David heard the giant speak,
And he felt bold and brave.
"By God's might I will win this fight.
By His strength we'll be saved!"

Saul, the king, gave all his armor,
But David turned it down.
"It's way too big and heavy,
And I cannot move around."

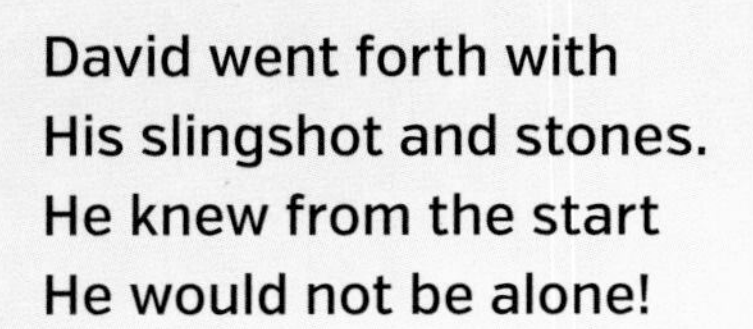

David went forth with
His slingshot and stones.
He knew from the start
He would not be alone!

"Goliath, you come
With two spears and a sword,
But I come to you
In the name of the Lord!"

David reached into
His bag for a stone,
Slinging it straight
At the giant!
Goliath was struck in the
Head and fell down—
A giant no longer defiant!

The Philistines saw
That their hero was dead.
They turned from
God's army and ran.
They saw that young David
Had God on his side—
Against Him no army
Can stand!

Bedtime Prayer
Dear God, with You on my side, I never have to be afraid!

Bedtime Prayer
Dear God, I love to sing
Your praises every day!

The Singing Shepherd

Psalm 150

David loved
To play the harp,
To worship God in song.
He praised Him
While he watched
The sheep—
He praised Him
All day long.

Let all that breathes
Sing to the Lord.
Let our voices
Praise Him too!
Always remember
How good God is
And all He's
Done for you!

David and Jonathan, Forever Friends

1 Samuel 18

God fills our lives
With many good things.
Some of the best
Are the friendships He brings!

David and Jonathan,
Friends from the start,
Loved to serve God
And did not want to part!

Jonathan gave David
His sword and his belt.
He wanted to show him
The love that he felt.

Friends help each other.
They're kind and they're true.
Can *you* name a good friend
Who God's given you?

Bedtime Prayer

Dear God, bless my friends. They are good gifts from You!

Bedtime Prayer
Dear God, I pray that You will give me understanding and help me do what is right.

Solomon's Prayer That Pleased God

1 Kings 3

There was a king named Solomon.
He was David's son.
He liked to pray,
Served God each day,
And slept when day was done.

Now one night,
As the king slept tight
Beneath a bright moonbeam,
God appeared to Solomon
In a special dream.

God said, "Ask for what you want—
Anything from Me."
Solomon said, "A wise king, Lord,
Is what I'd like to be!"

God was pleased with Solomon.
He showed him what to do.
And God said, "There will never be
A king as wise as you!"

Elijah, Prophet of Fire and Miracles

Miracle Bread and the Boy Who Lived Again

1 Kings 17

God sent Elijah
To see a poor widow
Who lived alone
With her son.
Elijah said, “Bring me
A piece of bread.”
She answered,
“But sir, I have none.”

She did not know
That God had sent him
To save both her and her son.
He told her the jars of
Flour and oil
Would keep filling
Until she was done!

The widow made bread,
And then *more* bread . . .
She fed them day after day.
Just like God said,
The jars filled up
In a miraculous way!

Bedtime Prayer

Dear God, You care for me in so many ways, and Your word is always true!

In time, the widow's
Son became sick.
Each day he grew
Worse and worse.
The widow cried out
To Elijah and said,
"Did you come here
To bring me this curse?"

Elijah said, "Put your
Son in my arms,"
For he had stopped
Breathing and died.
Three times Elijah
Prayed to God . . .
"Let the boy live!" he cried.

God heard Elijah
Cry out to Him—
He answered his prayer
Right away.
The widow knew *God*
Had healed her son.
She believed He was true
From that day!

Bedtime Prayer

Dear God, help me remember Your power is great and with me every day.

Fire from Heaven

1 Kings 18

God sent Elijah to visit King Ahab,
Who followed the prophets of Baal.
But now came the hour
To show him God's power,
Because it will never fail!

Two altars were built for a sacrifice.
The prophets of Baal went first.
They prayed and prayed . . .
The sacrifice stayed.
No spark or fire would burst.

Elijah said, "Maybe your god is asleep.
Pray louder to wake him up!"
The prophets prayed louder,
Their words became prouder,
Still, no flame would erupt.

It was Elijah's turn to pray:
God, hear my prayer so they'll know
That You have all power,
And You'll never cower.
All their idols must go!

Fire came down,
Burning altar and ground.
Everyone standing there knew:
The Lord God is best,
His people are blessed,
And all of His words are true!

Jonah, Stubborn and Swallowed!

Jonah 1–3

A prophet is someone
God speaks through—
To let people know
The right thing to do.
God told Jonah
To visit a place
Where there was not
One bit of good (not a trace)!

Nineveh didn't love God
As they should.
But He still loved them,
Because God's always good!
Jonah said, "Nope. I do *not*
Want to go.
The people of Nineveh
Don't need to know."

Jonah hopped onto a boat
Of his choice,
Ignoring God's message,
Ignoring God's voice.
Jonah forgot
He was only a man—
He had no power
To stop God's plan!

God sent a storm
To the boat Jonah chose.
The crew was afraid,
"Why is God mad? *Who knows?*"
Jonah said, "Me.
I'm why it was sent."
So into the wild, blue sea
Jonah went!

The minute that Jonah
Fell into the sea,
The wind and the waves
Were as calm as could be.
And just when this prophet
Was sure he would drown,
A giant fish
Swallowed him down!

A swoosh, a gulp . . .
A sad, soggy man.
Jonah was sorry
He ran from God's plan.
He spent three days
In the fish's round belly—
Slimy, slippery,
Goopy, and smelly.

Bedtime Prayer

Dear God, help me obey You, even when it's hard!

Jonah prayed, *God, I will*
Do what You say.
I know Your word
Is the only true way.
The giant fish burped,
Then came a *thump*.
Jonah rolled onto the beach
With a bump.

He went straight to Nineveh
As he was told.
He wasn't afraid.
He was brave and bold!
The people believed.
"We'll serve God *today*!"
They prayed and turned from
Their not-so-nice ways.

Bedtime Prayer
Dear God, Your love is so big! Thank You for sending a Savior!

Isaiah Tells of the Coming King

Isaiah 9

Isaiah was a prophet
Who announced
God's greatest plan—
One day the world
Would meet a King
Who'd be both
God and man.

His love would stretch
Across the sky
And fill the oceans blue.
His love would heal
What's broken
And make our hearts
Brand-new.

Prince of Peace!
Wonderful!
Son of God is He.
He'll come to earth,
From heaven's home,
To rescue you and me.

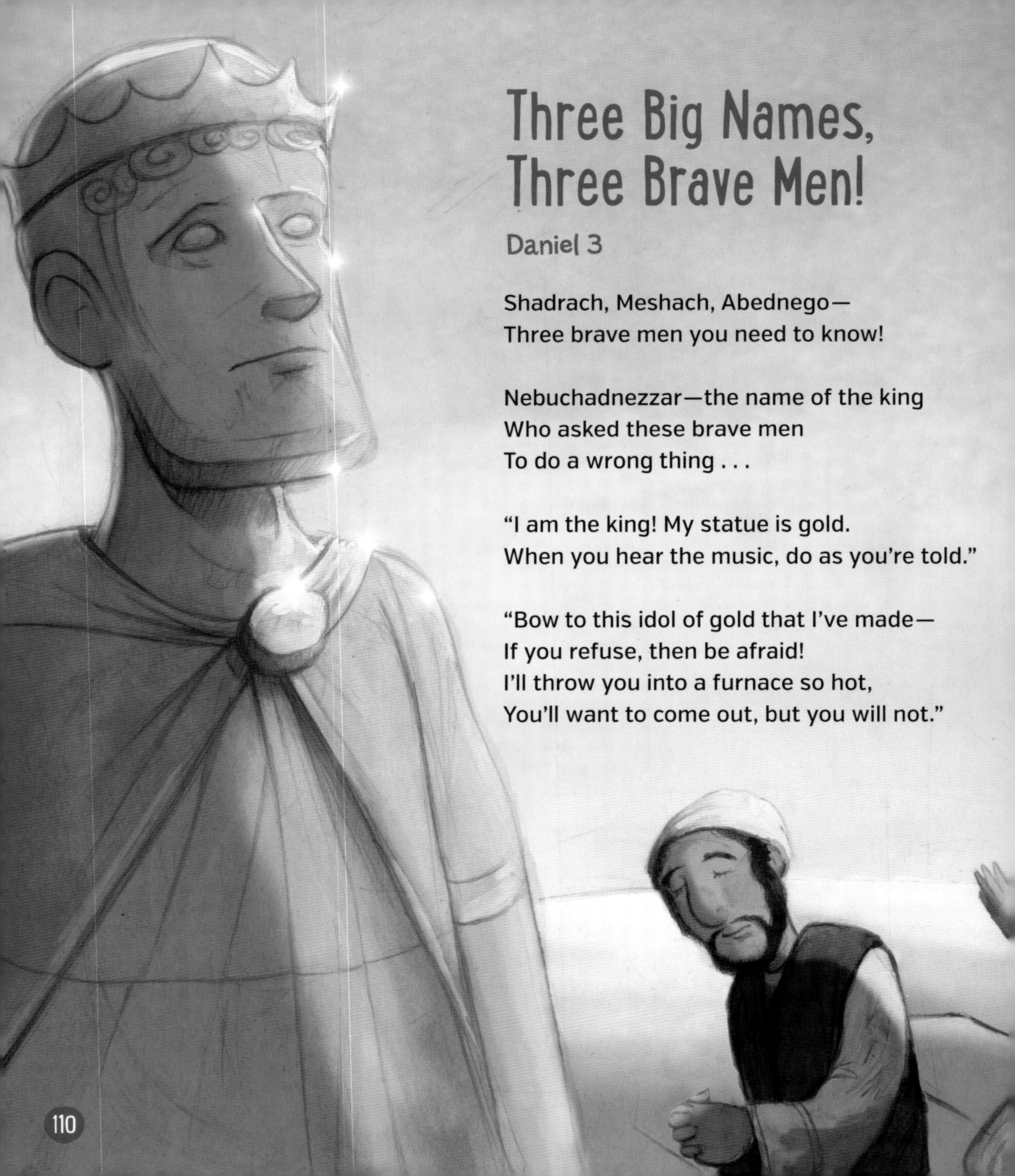

Three Big Names, Three Brave Men!

Daniel 3

Shadrach, Meshach, Abednego—
Three brave men you need to know!

Nebuchadnezzar—the name of the king
Who asked these brave men
To do a wrong thing . . .

"I am the king! My statue is gold.
When you hear the music, do as you're told."

"Bow to this idol of gold that I've made—
If you refuse, then be afraid!
I'll throw you into a furnace so hot,
You'll want to come out, but you will not."

Shadrach, Meshach,
And Abednego
Told the king flatly,
“This you should know:
We’ll never bow to a
Statue you make.
God’s able to save us.
Our faith you can’t shake!”

Bedtime Prayer
Dear God, I'm thankful You protect me every day.

King Nebuchadnezzar
Kept his word.
The brave men
Kept theirs too.
The music played . . .
They didn't bow.
"Let's see if your
God will save you!"

"Heat up the furnace
Seven times hotter,
Then throw these
Men in today.
I am the king!
I make the rules.
My servants
Must do as I say!"

Shadrach, Meshach,
And Abednego
Were tied up and
Thrown in the flames.
The king looked into
The furnace and shouted,
"I thought I gave
You *three* names!"

Clearly, *four* men
Were in the fire.
The Lord came to
Save them all!
The king proclaimed,
"Their God is great.
Against Him
All others will fall!"

Daniel Sleeps in the Lions' Den

Daniel 4–6

Daniel loved God with all of his heart;
His love for God set him apart.
He worked very hard to serve the king,
And he was blessed in everything!

Other men grumbled—they were mad
Because of the favor Daniel had.
The king liked Daniel most of all.
The others wanted to see him fall.

They tricked the king into making a law
To punish anybody they saw
Worshipping any person or thing
Other than their mighty king.

But Daniel kept praying three times a day—
He worshipped and honored God that way.
The leaders spied and told the king,
"Punish Daniel! He's doing the wrong thing!"

These men who spied
With their sneaky eyes
Upset the king with their
Sudden surprise.
"But you signed the law
With your very own pen.
Now throw Daniel
Into the lions' den!"

The king was sad
And fearful and mad.
"Daniel's the greatest
Leader I've had!"
But a law is a rule,
No matter how cruel,
And the lions were pacing
About as they drooled . . .

They threw Daniel into
The lion-filled den
And put a large stone
Where the entrance had been.
The king didn't sleep.
He worried and cried
And hoped Daniel's God
Wouldn't let him die.

The night finally passed.
The morning came
As the king reached the den
And called Daniel's name.

The king heard a voice
Shout from inside.
"Your majesty!"
Daniel quickly replied.
"My God sent an angel
To close their jaws,
So I slept safely
In the lions' paws!"

The king was excited,
As pleased as could be,
"Hear this!" he announced,
"It is plain to see:
The God Daniel serves
Is mighty and great!
He saves His people,
And He's never late."

Bedtime Prayer
Dear God, I praise You because You are mighty and great! Your love makes me feel safe.

Dear God, show me the special gifts You've given me to help others.

Nehemiah, a Builder to the Rescue

Nehemiah 1–8

God gives His children
Special gifts,
Things they'll be
Very good at.
Israel needed a
Builder to help them,
So God delivered
Just that!

God gave the prophet
Nehemiah
Something important
To do:
"The walls of Jerusalem
Have been knocked down,
And the one to rebuild
Them is you!"

Nehemiah happily
Used his skills
To help rebuild
The walls.
One day you'll
Use *your* special gifts
To help the world
When God calls!

Brave Queen Esther

Esther 1–8

There once was a king
In search of a queen.
Many girls gathered
So they could be seen.
A young Jewish girl,
Her beauty like art,
Caught the king's eye
And captured his heart.

The king chose her swiftly
And crowned her Queen Esther.
God wanted her there,
Where the king's favor blessed her.
Her cousin named Mordecai
Worked for the king
And heard he was
Planning a very bad thing.

The king's servant, Haman,
Who wasn't so nice,
Had gone to the king
With some awful advice:

"Those who won't bow to you—
They're called Jews—
Let them all die!
You're in charge, so they lose!"

The king agreed that
The Israelites must go.
But there was a secret
The king did not know . . .

Queen Esther was one of them.
She would die too!
But God gave her courage
For what she must do.

She prayed for her people
And knew in her heart
God's goodness would save them,
And she'd do her part.

Esther was wise, and
She followed God's plan.
Bravely she went to the king.
He welcomed her,
Though she'd taken a risk,
Not knowing he'd give her a thing!

He held out his scepter
[A greeting of favor]
And asked her, "What's your request?
Half of my kingdom
Is yours if you'd like,"
But Esther felt this way was best:

For two nights she planned
A great feast for the king.
The second night, she would reveal
That Haman had worked out
A terrible plan—
The life of her people to steal.

"What's this?!" roared the king
As he crushed Haman's plan.
God's people now lived without fear!
God will be faithful to *you*
When you pray . . .
His great love will always be near.

Bedtime Prayer
Dear God, You are always faithful,
and Your love is with me every day.

New Testament Stories

God's people squabbled
And wobbled and fell.
God rescued them,
Leaving great stories to tell—
Of battles won,
Miracles done,
And prophets who spoke of
God sending His Son.

The time had come
For our Savior's birth,
For Jesus to bring
God's love to earth.
His love is still here,
His presence near.
With Him in our hearts
We can live without fear.

Mary and the Birth of Our King

Surprised by an Angel

Luke 1

Mary, a young girl from Galilee,
Had started her usual day,
When suddenly, God sent a message
To her in a surprising way.

Poof! An angel, covered in light,
Was standing in front of her!
He said, “I am Gabriel. Don’t be afraid—
God has *blessed* you. You can be sure.”

He told her she’d have a baby boy,
And Jesus would be His name.
The Savior, the King, the Son of God—
There would never be one the same!

Mary said, “I will serve the Lord
And do what He asks me to do.”
So Jesus was on His way to earth
To rescue me and you!

A Cradle of Hay

Luke 2

Joseph and Mary,
Engaged to be married,
Were told of the emperor's call—
Caesar Augustus said,
"Count the people.
This goes for one and all!"

Bethlehem,
Joseph's family home,
The place they traveled to,
Had no rooms
To rent for the night.
A stable would have to do.

The time had come
For the birth of God's Son,
Among the cows and sheep.
Mary wrapped Jesus
In simple cloth
And laid Him down to sleep.

A cradle of hay
Seems like a poor bed
To hold a heavenly King . . .
But God knew the world
Would need to see
That *love* is the greatest thing.

Dear God, thank You for sending
Your Son, our heavenly King!

Bedtime Prayer

Dear God, thank You for Jesus,
the best gift of all!

Shepherds Hear the Good News

Luke 2

God wanted the whole
Wide world to know
How *big* His love can be!
It's not just for kings
Or fancy folks—
It's for everyone's heart to see.

So He sent the news
To lowly shepherds
That Jesus had come to earth.
An angel appeared,
Glowing like the sun.
"I'm here to announce His birth!"

The shepherds jumped back—
They were so afraid.
But the angel calmed all their fear.
"I bring good news
To all the earth:
The Savior is finally here!"

The pasture filled up
With angels saying,
"Glory to God on high!"
The shepherds ran off
To Bethlehem
To see Him with their own eyes.

Bedtime Prayer

Dear God, Your love shines down on me all day and through the night.

A Star Lights the Way for Wise Men

Matthew 2

God hung a silver star in place
The night our King came down.
It shined the brightest beam of love
Upon that little town.

Even from a far-off land
The light was clearly seen.
Some wise men saw the star and smiled.
They knew what it must mean.

"God has sent the promised King,
And we must go to Him!"
Throughout their hard and lengthy trip,
The star did not go dim.

At last they entered Bethlehem
And found the tiny place
Where Love was born—the King of kings
With starlight on His face.

John the Baptist and the Voice from Heaven

Luke 1, 3

Jesus' cousin, John the Baptist,
Helped to spread the word:
"The Savior's come to take your sin!"
He baptized those who heard.

One day, Jesus came to John—
He wanted baptism too.
But John did not feel worthy
Of what he was asked to do!

Jesus told him *God* decides
The way that things should go.
As soon as John obeyed his
Master, God would let him know . . .

The sky burst open! Light streamed down!
A great voice thundered out!
"You're My Son. I'm pleased with You,"
Proclaimed God with a shout.

A white dove touched down gently,
And the faith around Him grew:
Jesus is the Son of God!
He's come to make us new!

Bedtime Prayer

Dear God, thank You for giving me friends and family who teach me Your ways.

Jesus Chooses His Helpers

Luke 5 and Mark 3

Jesus began to talk and teach
About God's wonderful plan.
"I'm here to save the world from sin . . .
The only One who can."

He taught from a
Fisherman's boat one day
Along the sandy shore.
Andrew and Peter
Had fished all night;
They did not want to try anymore.

Jesus said, "Row your boat
Out again, and let down
Your nets for a catch."
They listened, and soon
They had their fish—
A net-ripping, boat-tipping batch!

Andrew, Peter, James, and John,
Amazed at what He had done,
Left their nets to follow Jesus.
They knew He must be God's Son!

Twelve men chose
To follow Jesus,
Learning more
Each day
Of God's great plan
To save us—
How He'd wash
Our sins away.

Bartholomew,
And Thaddaeus,
Another James,
(That's two) . . .
Philip, Thomas,
Judas, Simon,
Matthew
(Now we're through!).

When we choose
To follow Jesus,
He can teach *us* too.
If we pray and
Read His Word,
He'll show us
What to do!

Bedtime Prayer

Dear God, I want to follow You and learn more about You every day.

Bedtime Prayer
Dear God, I'm happy to be Your child.
I want to please You every day!

Jesus the Teacher

Beatitudes: Good Ways to Be

Matthew 5

Jesus sat down
To teach one day,
And the people
Gathered around.
A mountain became
A meeting place—
Not an empty spot
Could be found!

"Be sorry for sin,
Be sad to do wrong,
Be one who serves God
With your heart.
Be helpful to others,
Forgive and be kind,
Don't follow the world—
Stand apart."

"Others will know
You're a child of God,
Happy inside
And blessed.
I'll be with you.
I'll be your Friend.
I'll help you
Be your best!"

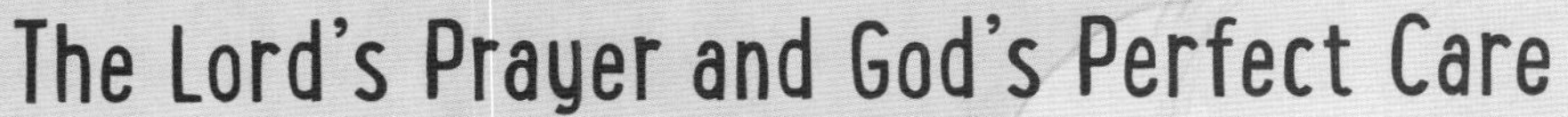

The Lord's Prayer and God's Perfect Care

Matthew 6

Talking with God
In prayer is good!
Jesus taught us
To pray like we should:

"Father in heaven,
Your name is great!
Make earth a place
Of love, not hate.
Provide the things
We need today.
Forgive our sins,
We humbly pray."

And Jesus taught
Another thing:
To watch the birds
Who fly and sing.
They never worry,
Fret, or fuss . . .
And God cares
Even *more* for us!

Just look at how
The flowers grow,
Putting on their
Vibrant show,
Dressed in colors
Fit for kings,
Without a thought
Of doing a thing!

God cares for *you*
This perfect way
And sees the things
You need each day.
He watches as you
Grow and play
And listens closely
When you pray.

Bedtime Prayer

Dear God, thank You for Your always-there, always-perfect care!

Bedtime Prayer
Dear God, I love You with all my heart, and Your love helps me love others too.

The Most Important Thing to Do

Matthew 22

Lots of people came to Jesus,
Asking lots of things.
"What's the greatest message
That the law of Moses brings?"

Jesus said, "Love God the most!
With joy and all your heart!
Then show love to others,
And let that be just a start."

Everything you say and do,
Everything you must go through,
Everyone you bump into—
Sprinkle with God's love!

Every friend who needs a hand,
Every job (both small and grand),
Things you don't quite understand—
Treat with God's great love!

The Shepherd Cares for the Lost

Luke 15

It never feels good
To be lost or left out.
It makes Jesus sad to see.
We are His sheep.
He is our Shepherd.
With Him is where we should be.

If one of His sheep,
Just one little one,
Wanders away from His side,
He won't give up!
He won't give in!
He'll search both far and wide.

When Jesus finds
The one who's lost,
He sings a happy song!
"My lamb is safe now
In My arms,
Where all My sheep belong!"

Bedtime Prayer

Dear God, keep me safe in Your arms and close to Your side.

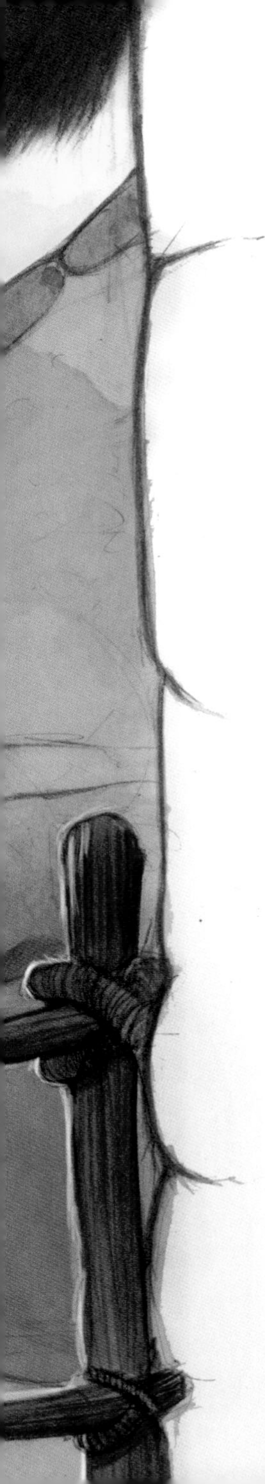

The Runaway Son and a Father's Forgiveness

Luke 15

There once was a father
Raising two sons.
They worked together
To get the chores done.
One day the young son
Grumbled and said,
"I'm bored being here.
I'll travel instead."

His father was sad
As he watched his son go.
Would he come back?
There was no way to know.
The son felt happy,
Excited, and free.
He thought, *How fun*
This adventure will be!

He spent every bit
Of the money he had
On things quite foolish
And friends who were bad.
Then he got hungry,
Lonely, and sad.
"If I go home,
Will Father be mad?"

Afraid to go home,
He settled for less.
He took a job feeding pigs—
What a mess!
The farmer he worked for
Was not in the mood
To care for his workers
Or give them some food.

The runaway son
Couldn't run any more.
His stomach was growling
Like never before.

"I have to go home now.
This isn't so fun!
I'm sorry for all of the
Bad things I've done."

The son headed home.
He was hungry and poor.
He'd realized his father
Had given *much* more . . .

A safe place to rest,
A love that was best,
A home that was cozy
And comfy and blessed.

As soon as his father
Could see his young son,
He ran out to meet him.
The waiting was done!

"My son has returned.
We will feast and rejoice!
He's home with his father.
He's made the right choice!"

Bedtime Prayer

Dear God, when I'm sorry for my sin, You forgive me. Thank You for being a loving Father.

Bedtime Prayer
Dear God, I want to do good and show Your love by helping others.

The Good Samaritan: Love Is Helping Others

Luke 10

Jesus told a story
Of how love is what we *do*.
When we help someone in need,
God's love comes shining through.

A man was badly hurt.
He was left beside the road.
The robbers who had been there
Figured they'd just turn and go!

A man walked by and did not stop.
A second strolled right past.
A third man, a Samaritan,
Stopped to help at last!

He bandaged up the helpless man
And brought him to an inn.
There he took good care of him
So healing could begin.

Jesus asked, "Who loved his
Neighbor—proving he loves Me?"
The good Samaritan, of course!
It's how we all should be!

Dinner for Five Thousand, Please!

Mark 6, John 6

As Jesus kept teaching
And loving and healing,
He wanted some time
For a rest, He was feeling.
He told His disciples
To hop in a boat,
And off to a quieter
Place they would float.

Oh my! When they
Got to the quieter spot,
The people were waiting,
And there were *a lot*.
So Jesus decided to
Teach them all day.
Then the disciples said,
"Send them away!"

"It's dinnertime now,
And there's not enough food.
If we eat and they don't,
That would be rude!"
"Bring Me the food that
You have, and you'll see
How faithful My Father
In heaven will be."

A little boy's lunch
Of fishes and bread
Was given to Jesus.
And then Jesus said,
"Thank You, Father,
For Your loving care."
The few loaves and fishes
Fed *everyone* there!

Bedtime Prayer

Dear God, when I trust You and give thanks, I always have enough!

Bedtime Prayer
Dear God, I want to follow You and learn more about You every day.

Master of the Wild Waves

Luke 8

One day Jesus told His disciples,
"Let's sail out and get away."
They climbed into a fishing boat,
Being quick to show they'd obey.

Their Master, Jesus, fell asleep,
Peaceful, quiet, carefree.
The sails were set to cross the sea,
But the weather would disagree.

The wind, it howled; the waves, they growled.
The thunder and lightning crashed down!
"Master!" they cried. "You must wake up.
We're afraid we're all going to drown!"

Jesus stood up, as calm as could be,
And said, "Be still!" to the angry sea.
Then, just as suddenly as it had started,
The scary storm at once departed.

Jesus said, "Why were you all so afraid?
Where is your *trust* in Me?"
The disciples, amazed, and slightly dazed,
Said, "He even commands the sea!"

A Watery Walk

Matthew 14

Jesus went up on a
Hillside to pray.
He told His disciples
To make their way
Into a boat to cross the sea.
He'd catch up eventually.

Their boat was afloat
Through the night.
The water was deep,
No land in sight.
The waves were swelling.
The wind was yelling.
How long it would last,
There was no telling.

A flash of lightning
Lit up the night.
They saw someone coming—
It filled them with fright.
"A ghost," they cried,
"Who walks on the sea!"

"Don't be afraid!"
Jesus shouted. "It's Me!"

Peter said, “Lord, if that’s true,
I’ll leave this boat and walk to You.”
Peter walked, wave to wave,
Then got scared and not so brave.
Peter cried out—Jesus grabbed his hand.
Alone he’d sink . . . but with Jesus, he’d stand!

Bedtime Prayer

Dear God, trusting You is the best way to be brave. I’m happy You are always with me!

Bedtime Prayer
Dear God, I pray I'll always love and trust You, even when I'm grown up!

Children Have a Special Place

Matthew 19

Jesus spent lots of time
Showing God's love.
The disciples thought
He was worn out . . .
From teaching all day,
From telling great stories,
From healing
And walking about.

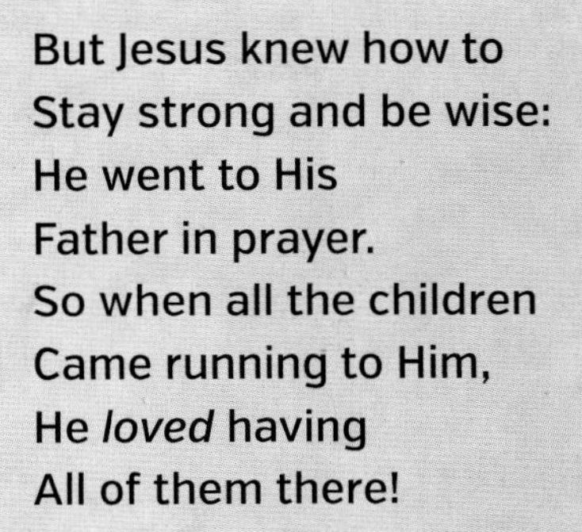

But Jesus knew how to
Stay strong and be wise:
He went to His
Father in prayer.
So when all the children
Came running to Him,
He *loved* having
All of them there!

His followers said,
"Leave our Master alone.
He's tired from
Such a long day."
Jesus corrected them,
"Let them come!
Do not send the
Children away."

And so they laughed
And talked
And played.
Jesus taught
This lesson too:
"If you want to make heaven
Your home one day,
Love Me like children do!"

The Savior Visits Mary and Martha

Luke 10

Martha kept a lovely home,
Always very clean.
If you saw it, you might say
It's the neatest you've ever seen.

Jesus came into town one day.
Martha invited Him in.
"Lord, please stay as long as You'd like!"
Then she had chores to begin.

Her sister, Mary, sat with Jesus,
Listening and learning with care.
Martha was busy sweeping and dusting,
Scurrying here and there.

Martha's face was turning red,
Partly from rushing around,
Also because she was getting mad.
Her sister was sitting down!

Martha said, "Lord, I'm working away
While Mary sits with You!"
Jesus said, "Martha, you're too upset.
She chose the right thing to do."

Jesus wanted Martha to see
Time with Him is *best*.
It keeps us loving, wise, and kind,
Making our lives more blessed!

Bedtime Prayer
Dear God, please help me make good choices and spend time with You every day.

Jesus the Healer

A Little Girl Gets Well

Luke 8

More and more people
Were happy to hear
What Jesus, God's Son, could do.
He healed the sick!
He calmed the storm!
He showed God's love was true!

A man named Jairus
Had a young daughter
Who couldn't get well on her own.
Jairus believed that
Jesus would help.
He'd heard of the miracles shown.

Jairus knelt down
At Jesus' feet and told Him his
Daughter was ill.
He asked if Jesus
Would come to his home.
Jesus answered, "I will."

They got there and went
To the little girl's bed,
And Jesus held her hand.
She had stopped breathing,
But when Jesus spoke,
She was healed at His command!

Bedtime Prayer
Dear God, You are the great Healer.
Thank You for taking good care of me.

Bedtime Prayer
Dear God, You are good in all Your ways! I can always trust in You.

A Blind Man Sees

Mark 8

One day a blind man
Was brought to Jesus.
The village was busy
That day,
But Jesus was willing
To heal the man—
In a most unusual way.

He led the blind man
Out of the village,
Then Jesus spit on his eyes.
He asked the man if
He could see.
His answer was
Quite a surprise!

"Yes," the man answered.
"I can see people. They look
Like trees walking around."
There's no way that Jesus
Would leave him like that,
To go back and stroll
Through the town!

He put His hands on
Those eyes once more,
Then asked him if he could see.
The man answered,
"I can see clearly now,
And things are the way
They should be!"

Bedtime Prayer

Dear God, I praise You for Your mighty miracles and never-ending love!

Hello Again, Lazarus!

John 11

Mary and Martha had a brother—
Lazarus was his name.
They loved him a lot. Then one day he caught
A sickness and wasn't the same.

They sent for Jesus, who loved him too.
Lazarus was His friend.
The Lord didn't worry or get in a hurry.
God's power doesn't end.

He waited days, two days too many—
The sickness got worse and won.
Lazarus died. Everyone cried,
Sure their hope was gone.

Jesus arrived at the heartbreaking scene:
Lazarus inside a tomb.
Jesus shed tears, Calmed their fears,
Then ended all their gloom.

"Move the stone. Push it away!"
It started a great-God-of-miracles day.
With the Lord's shout: "Lazarus, come out!"
God chased their sadness away.

Lazarus rose! Lazarus lived!
Joy returned to their days.
Death lost. Life won.
Let's give God the praise!

Zacchaeus, a Little Man with a Big Sorry

Luke 19

Zacchaeus collected taxes
And collected more than he should.
He took what people owed, then took more.
That's *stealing* (and that's *not good*).

Like everyone else, he longed to see Jesus,
But he was as short as could be.
The crowd kept crowding and stood very tall,
So he climbed a sycamore tree.

What a great view! he thought to himself,
Then realized that Someone was there . . .
Standing below him with soft, kind eyes,
Jesus met his stare.

"Let's go to your home," Jesus said,
And Zacchaeus quickly obeyed.
During their visit, his heart was changed.
He felt sorry for those he betrayed.

"I'll give it all back," he told the Lord.
"What I stole and three times more!"
Jesus was happy—this man felt new.
That's what He came to earth for!

Bedtime Prayer
Dear God, help me to do what's right
and say I'm sorry when I'm wrong.

Bedtime Prayer

Dear God, thank You for giving us Your Son, the King of kings!

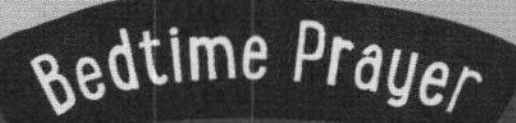

Palm Sunday: Jesus Goes to Jerusalem

John 12

Jesus knew the time was near
To save the world from sin.
Jerusalem is where God said
His life would have to end.

He rode a donkey through the gates,
Where people gave a cheer.
They shouted, "Bless the King of kings!"
"Praise God, He's finally here!"

They waved palm branches in the air
And laid some on the ground.
But soon the leaders of the town
Would not want Him around.

The Last Supper

Mark 14

The time had come for Passover,
A time to think about
The way God's people slaved in Egypt
And how God brought them out!

The disciples sat at a big table,
And Jesus broke the bread.
"My body will be broken too
For all the world," He said.

Then He shared that someone there,
A follower and friend,
Would give Him to His enemies,
And soon His life would end.

The disciples were sad,
But Jesus told them
This was God's great plan.
He had to die to take our sins
So we'd be new again.

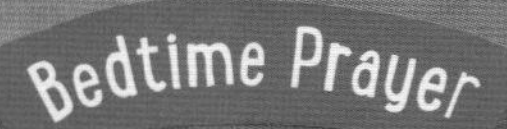

Bedtime Prayer

Dear God, I love You for making a way to save the world by giving Your only Son.

Jesus Prays in the Garden

Mark 14–15

Jesus told His disciples,
"You'll lose faith in Me."
Peter shouted, "No, I won't!"
And yet, it came to be.

They followed Jesus to a garden,
Where the Lord could pray.
He walked ahead to be alone,
Telling a few to stay.

Judas snuck away to do
The bad thing he had planned,
To lead the ones who hated Jesus
To the Son of Man.

Jesus was arrested
By a group of angry men.
They took Him to a crowded place.
His suffering would begin . . .

Pilate was the governor
Who put the Lord on trial.
The crowds were growing angrier,
Shouting all the while.

"Hang Him on the cross to die!
That's what we want done!"
Just as God had promised,
We'd be saved by His own Son.

Bedtime Prayer

Dear God, I pray I will always follow You and do what You have planned for me.

Good Friday: Jesus Dies on the Cross

Matthew 27

Soldiers put a robe on Jesus,
Then a crown of thorns.
They were making fun of Him
Amid the people's scorns.

They led Him from the city
To a place up on a hill.
Nailing Him upon the cross,
The soldiers mocked Him still.

They put a sign above His head
That said "King of the Jews."
People walked by teasing Him
(An awful thing to choose).

At noon the sky turned dark as night
And stayed that way three hours.
A missing sun was not the norm—
It had to be God's power!

Jesus cried out to His Father,
"Why have You left Me?"
God had turned from all our sin.
This sad thing had to be.

Hurting, lonely, sad, and bleeding,
Jesus died that day.
But God had promised long ago
It wouldn't end this way!

Bedtime Prayer

Dear God, Your plans are always perfect, just like Your love.

Easter Sunday: Jesus Is Alive!

Matthew 27-28 and John 20

A rich man named Joseph
Came into town,
Offering a tomb for the King.
He wrapped Jesus' body in cloth.
This man did a very kind thing.

Bedtime Prayer

Dear God, I'm thankful my sins are forgiven and I have new life because of Jesus!

Day one, the tomb
Was sealed with a stone.
Day two, it was guarded.
Day three, it was a busy place
The moment sunrise started.

Some women went there
With jars of perfume
And found an amazing surprise!
The stone was moved
Away from the tomb.
A bright light blinded their eyes.

An angel sat on top of the stone,
Outshining the sun and the moon.
"You're looking for Jesus,"
He said with a smile.
"He's risen! You'll see Him soon!"

The women went to the disciples,
But they had trouble believing . . .
Till Jesus walked into
The room they were in,
To find them all doubting and grieving.

Jesus Goes Back to Heaven

Matthew 28, Acts 1

Jesus' followers loved every minute
Spent with their risen Lord.
But He had to leave for their work to begin.
They'd never have time to be bored!

"Tell the whole world I love them always.
I died on the cross for their sin.
Now they can live forever in heaven.
My Father will let them in!"

"I'm going to prepare a home for you,
Where you will live one day.
The happiest place, without a sad face.
Every tear is wiped away!"

His followers felt the *best* feeling inside
As they stood on top of the hill.
They looked at the sky filled with light
And stood there, very still.

Just like a feather floating on air,
Jesus rose up and away . . .
Through clouds so bright and sparkling white.
He promised to return one day!

Bedtime Prayer

Dear God, thank You for making a way for me to go to heaven and preparing a home for me there!

God Sends a Helper and Friend

Acts 2

Before Jesus left to live in heaven,
He said, "I won't leave you alone.
My Father is planning to send you a Friend.
His love will be just like My own!"

The disciples gathered inside a room.
They heard a great noise moving through.
It roared like a wind only heaven could send,
Doing what only God's hand could do!

The rushing wind brought flames of fire.
Above every head they burned.
Then suddenly God's power filled them up.
They spoke languages they'd never learned!

Their hearts were joyful, thankful, and blessed.
The great Holy Spirit was there!
They went out to teach about Jesus, the Savior.
With Him there is no need to fear!

Bedtime Prayer

Dear God, thank You for the Holy Spirit, my Helper and Friend!

God's Church—Open to the World!

Acts 2–3

The church is not just a building
With windows, doors, and walls.
The church is made of *people* too—
People who answer God's call.

The ones who were serving Jesus
Began to share the good news.
They told the crowds who listened to them
God's love is what they should choose!

The disciples traveled together,
Going from here to there.
They sold all their belongings
So they could continue to share.

Thousands of people believed the truth
And what Jesus Christ had done.
The bad people thought they killed Him,
But God's perfect love had won!

Bedtime Prayer

Dear God, I pray I'll be brave and loving every day so others can learn about Your love.

Bedtime Prayer

Dear God, Your power is greater than anything on earth! Thank You for sharing it with me.

Jumping for Joy

Acts 1, 3

Jesus told His followers,
"You'll have My power too!
Miracles I've done for others,
You'll begin to do."

John and Peter, going to pray,
Passed the temple gate.
A man who begged for money
Lay there in a crippled state.

He looked at them with pleading eyes.
Then Peter boldly said,
"We have no gold or silver,
But a better gift instead."

"In Jesus' name and by His power,
Stand up now and walk."
The man stood up! His legs were strong!
These words were not just talk.

He jumped for joy, with shouts of praise!
This gift had changed his heart.
He went into the temple,
Thanking God for his new start!

An Ethiopian Hears the Happy News

Acts 8

Jesus' followers traveled,
For they had much to do,
Telling people God loves them—
He would save them too!

An angel came to Philip
With a different way to go.
"God said you should now go south.
I came to let you to know."

A chariot sat upon the road
And held a fine-dressed man
Reading from the Scripture.
Philip said, "Do you understand?"

The man said, "I don't understand."
And Philip said, "I'll teach you."
He taught of Jesus and His love
And what He came to do.

This man from Ethiopia
Was thrilled at Philip's teaching.
God had sent him on that road
For one man He was reaching!

That's how much God cares for us—
His love is *everywhere*!
If He sees one heart in need,
His love will be right there!

Bedtime Prayer
Dear God, Your love reaches everywhere
and is always with me. Help me share it!

Dear God, thank You for choosing me to do great things for You!

Saul's Change of Heart (and Name)

Acts 9

Saul of Tarsus set out for Damascus.
He got there, but wasn't the same.
Saul wasn't the nicest,
Yet God thought him priceless.
(He's known by a different name.)

On his way to Damascus,
Saul stopped in his tracks—
A light from above showered down.
"Saul, why do you hurt Me?"
"The Lord? *Can it be?*"
Shaking, Saul fell to the ground.

Three days without seeing
Made Saul start believing
That Jesus was God's only Son.
He met Ananias,
Who prayed for his sight.
Saul's work for the Lord had begun.

The apostle Paul, once known as Saul,
Was chosen by God for great things.
He soon would be teaching
A message far-reaching—
To people, priests, and kings!

Paul's Prison Letters

God Wants Us to Think Good Things!

Philippians 4

Paul was a leader,
The very best kind.
He loved God and always
Had others in mind.
Even from prison,
He wrote to his friends
Of how Jesus' goodness
And love never ends!

He cheered on others
With his many good words,
Hoping he'd help
Them to see
That gentle, loving,
Generous, and kind,
Is how they should
Try to be!

Paul said, "Try to think
About only good things . . .
Stay happy about all
The blessings God brings!
Pray all the time,
Thanking God when you start.
And learn to live life
With an unselfish heart."

Bedtime Prayer

Dear God, I love to talk with You
and learn how to be good and kind.

God's Always-True, Always-There Love

Ephesians 2–3

Paul loved to teach
About God's love for *you*.
He understood well,
For he needed it too.

Each day when you wake up
And open your eyes,
These two things should
Never be a surprise:

God loves you,
As sure as the moon
Moves the tide,
As high as the sky,
The whole universe wide,
As deep as an ocean
Without any bottom.
You can't do a thing
That would slow Him
Or stop Him.

God made you,
For dreams that are
Just right for you,
The special
And marvelous
Things that you'll do.
Imagine away,
Every night, every day.
You love God right back
Every time that you pray.

Bedtime Prayer

Dear God, I praise You for Your love—the always-true, always-there love I can count on.

Young Timothy Shares Jesus' Love

Acts 16

Timothy was a young man
Who loved God with all his heart.
The men who followed Jesus
Saw that God set him apart.

Paul invited Timothy
To travel and to share
About the new life Jesus brings
And God's unending care.

They met a girl named Lydia
Who listened to them speak.
She loved the Lord and knew they
Had the truth that all hearts seek.

She and her whole family
Welcomed all they had to say.
They were baptized, filled with joy,
And thankful for that day!

God can use each one of us,
The big, the tall, the small,
If He sees and knows
Our hearts will love Him most of all!

Bedtime Prayer
Dear God, I pray Your love will give me the courage to tell others about all You've done!

Peter Set Free!

Acts 12

Peter was in prison—
King Herod put him there,
Just for teaching: "Jesus lives!"
It gave the king a scare.

The thing King Herod didn't know
Is that God always wins!
After all, He saved the world—
His Son took all our sins!

While Peter sat inside his cell,
The room was filled with light . . .
An angel stood before him,
Sent to set him free that night!

His chains fell off,
His shoes went on,
And through the gates he ran!
Then Peter went to his
Friend's house
To praise the God
Who *can* . . .

Save us, free us,
Love us, help us.
He's our greatest Hero!
God will be right
By our side,
No matter where we go.

Bedtime Prayer
Dear God, You are my biggest
Hero. I can always count on You.

Bedtime Prayer

Dear God, thank You for Your promise of heaven—our perfect, *forever* home!

The Best Place Ever, for Our Forever!

Revelation 1, 21, 22

God has a plan and things go as they should,
Wrapped in His love and amazingly good.
John got a peek at where we will live,
The place our Father is happy to give!

Heaven! The city that's brighter than bright,
Where Jesus is King, and Love is our light.
Where gates are great pearls,
The streets are gold swirls,
And walls are a colorful sight!

Tears? There aren't any.
Smiles? There are many!
Singing floats sweetly on air.
Jesus will come and make this our new home!
We'll be like a family there.

Jesus told John, "I'm the First and the Last.
One day, all troubles will be in the past.
My people will be in God's presence with Me."
Come quickly, Lord Jesus. We can't wait to see!

Everything on earth,
shout with joy to God!

—Psalm 66:1